S0-AGM-016

Disney PRINCESS

Tangled

Read-Along
STORYBOOK AND CD

When Rapunzel meets Flynn Rider, the pair travel across the kingdom. To find out what happens, read along with me in your book. You will know it's time to turn the page when you hear this sound. . . .

Let's begin now.

Published by Disney Press, an imprint of Disney Book Group.
No part of this book may be reproduced or transmitted in any form or by any means, electronic or mechanical, including photocopying, recording, or by any information storage and retrieval system, without written permission from the publisher. For information address Disney Press, 1101 Flower Street, Glendale, California 91201.

Printed in the United States of America
First Bindup Edition, June 2017
1 3 5 7 9 10 8 6 4 2

Library of Congress Control Number: 2016938190
FAC-008598-17111
ISBN 978-1-4847-8780-9

For more Disney Press fun, visit www. disneybooks.com

Disney PRESS
Los Angeles • New York

SUSTAINABLE FORESTRY INITIATIVE

Certified Chain of Custody
At Least 20% Certified Forest Content
www.sfiprogram.org
SFI-00993

Logo Applies to Text Stock Only

Once there lived a king and queen. They were very happy together. When the Queen was expecting a baby, she fell ill. The King's men searched far and wide until they found a magical golden flower. The Queen was cured. Soon a golden-haired daughter was born.

Everyone celebrated—except an old woman named Mother Gothel.
She had used the Golden Flower for hundreds of years to keep from
aging. She was furious that it was gone. So she went to the castle.
Realizing the child's golden hair had the same magic as the flower,
she kidnapped her.

The girl was called Rapunzel. Mother Gothel raised her in a tower. She kept her hidden there for nearly eighteen years. "You must stay here, where you're safe." She said it was dangerous outside, but she actually wanted Rapunzel's magic hair for herself.

Rapunzel's hair grew so long that Mother Gothel used it to come and go from the tower. "Rapunzel! Let down your hair!"

Rapunzel would use her hair to pull up Mother Gothel.

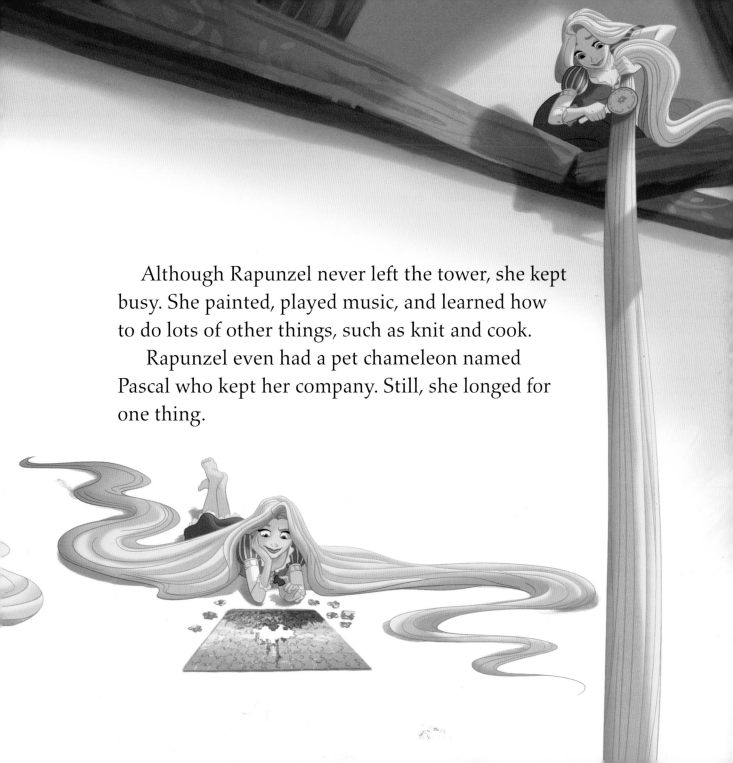

Although Rapunzel never left the tower, she kept busy. She painted, played music, and learned how to do lots of other things, such as knit and cook.

Rapunzel even had a pet chameleon named Pascal who kept her company. Still, she longed for one thing.

Each year on Rapunzel's birthday, floating lights filled the sky. Rapunzel desperately wanted to see them. She didn't know they were lanterns released by the King and Queen, who hoped their daughter would someday return. Rapunzel felt the lanterns were somehow meant for her. She even painted them on a tower wall.

Rapunzel begged Mother Gothel to see the lights for her eighteenth birthday. "I need to see them—in person. I have to know what they are."

Mother Gothel refused. "Don't ever ask to leave this tower again."

Soon Mother Gothel went out into the forest.

Meanwhile, a thief named Flynn Rider was nearby. The royal guards were chasing him, since he had a stolen crown in his bag.

The captain led the chase. "Retrieve that satchel at any cost!"

The captain's horse, Maximus, nearly caught Flynn, but the thief escaped. Flynn discovered Rapunzel's secret tower. He climbed up the outside, thinking he'd found the perfect place to hide.

Instead, Rapunzel knocked out Flynn with a frying pan. She tied him up and took the crown. Sure that this was her only chance to see the lights, she offered Flynn a deal: "You will act as my guide, take me to these lanterns, and return me home safely." Afterward she would give him the crown.

"Unfortunately, the kingdom and I aren't simpatico at the moment." But Flynn had no choice. "Fine, I'll take you to see the lanterns."

Flynn climbed down the tower, and Rapunzel used her hair
to leave. For the first time, her feet touched the grass. "I can't
believe I did this!" She felt as if her life was finally beginning.
"This is so fun!"

Flynn took Rapunzel to a pub, hoping to frighten her. "If you can't handle this place, maybe you should be back in your tower."

Instead, Rapunzel told a crowd of tough guys about the floating lights. "Because I've been dreaming about them my entire life!"

The men liked her. They shared their dreams, too.

Soon Mother Gothel returned to the tower. "Rapunzel! Let down your hair." Rapunzel didn't answer, so Mother Gothel went up the tower's hidden staircase. She found the stolen crown and a WANTED poster of Flynn. Mother Gothel set off to bring back Rapunzel.

Meanwhile, palace guards and Maximus suddenly arrived at
the pub. They were looking for Flynn. "Where's Rider? I know
he's in here somewhere! Find him!"

The men at the pub wanted Rapunzel to see the lights, so
one of them showed her and Flynn a secret tunnel. "Go live
your dream!"

The guards chased Rapunzel and Flynn. Rapunzel used her hair to help them escape, but the two became trapped in a cave. Water rushed in. Flynn could not find a way out. "I can't see anything."

Then Rapunzel admitted something. "I have magic hair that glows when I sing." She sang and her hair lit up the water.

They dove down and swam toward an opening.

They escaped at the last minute. "We made it. We're alive!"

Rapunzel noticed that Flynn's hand was cut. She wrapped it in her magic hair and sang.

Flynn could not believe it. Her hair had healed his hand. "How long has it been doing that exactly?" Rapunzel was different from anyone he'd ever met. The two talked for a while.

Meanwhile, Mother Gothel had tracked down Flynn and Rapunzel. She met the Stabbington brothers, two criminals who were after Flynn and the crown. "I was going to offer you something worth one thousand crowns."

Later Flynn went to get firewood, and Mother Gothel appeared. She had followed Rapunzel. "We're going home, Rapunzel. Now."

Rapunzel wouldn't leave. "I met someone. He likes me."

Mother Gothel dared Rapunzel to give Flynn the crown, sure that he would leave Rapunzel as soon as he had it.

"I will." Rapunzel agreed, but she took the crown and hid it.

The next morning was Rapunzel's birthday. Then Maximus showed up. Rapunzel convinced the horse not to take Flynn away. "Today is kind of the biggest day of my life. I need you not to get him arrested."

Soon they arrived in the city. The kingdom was celebrating the memory of their lost princess. Her birthday was the same as Rapunzel's.

Rapunzel saw a painting of the royal family. She felt as if she belonged there in the kingdom. When the townsfolk began to dance, Rapunzel and Flynn clasped hands and joined in. Later, they ate cake and went to shops together. It was a magical day. Rapunzel was very happy.

That evening, Flynn rowed Rapunzel into the harbor. "Well, best day of your life, I figure you should have a decent seat."

As the sky filled with lanterns, the pair realized they cared for each other. Rapunzel knew Flynn wouldn't leave her. She handed him the crown. "I should have given it to you before, but I was just scared."

Flynn saw the Stabbington brothers onshore. "There's just something I have to take care of." He gave the crown to the brothers, thinking they'd go away. Rapunzel was more important.

But the crown was not what they were after. "We want her instead."

The brothers tied up Flynn and sent him off in a boat. Then they told Rapunzel that Flynn had left with the crown. "A fair trade: a crown for the girl with the magic hair."

"What? No, he wouldn't!" Rapunzel was shocked.

The brothers tried to get Rapunzel, but she ran into the forest. When she heard a scuffle, she returned.

Mother Gothel was standing over the brothers. She had knocked them out. "Oh, my precious girl! Are you all right?" This was part of her cruel plan to get Rapunzel to return to the tower. "You were right, Mother. You were right about everything."

Back at the tower, Rapunzel kept thinking about the lanterns on her birthday and the portrait of the royal family. She looked at her paintings on the tower walls. Finally, it all started to make sense.

"I am the lost princess." Rapunzel realized that Mother Gothel had kept her prisoner. "And I will never let you use my hair again!"

Then Flynn arrived. Mother Gothel hurt him badly. But Flynn wouldn't let Rapunzel heal him. Instead he cut her magical hair so she would be free.

Mother Gothel was destroyed.

"You were my new dream." Flynn closed his eyes. He was gone.

Rapunzel wept, and a tear fell on Flynn. He was saved! There was magic in Rapunzel's tears, too.

Now that she was free, Rapunzel returned to the kingdom with Flynn, Maximus, and Pascal.

The King and Queen were overjoyed to see their daughter. Although Rapunzel's hair was no longer magical, she was happier from that day on than she could ever have dreamed.

Then it was time for the
reception—and time for Max and
Pascal to relax at last. That is, until
Max decided to rest his hoof on the
cart that held the royal wedding
cake. Before he knew it, the cart
began to roll away. Flynn hadn't
noticed. He spoke to the crowd.
"So, who wants a piece of cake?"

Little did he know that Max
and Pascal were about to have
another adventure. . . .

Stunned and distracted, the priest finished the ceremony. "I . . . I now pronounce you husband and wife. You may kiss."

And so Rapunzel and Flynn did, and the church instantly filled with cheers.

Rapunzel and Flynn had been gazing happily into
each other's eyes. But as they looked at Max and Pascal,
Rapunzel gasped. Flynn's jaw dropped open.

Everyone in the church stared at the ring bearers.
They couldn't imagine what had happened.

The rings were safe, and that was all that mattered. Max and Pascal raced back to the chapel, covered with tar and food, and wearing strange clothes. Luckily, the priest was just getting to the ring part.

". . . in everlasting peace. May I have the rings?"

Breathless, Max and Pascal held the rings up for the priest to give to Rapunzel and Flynn.

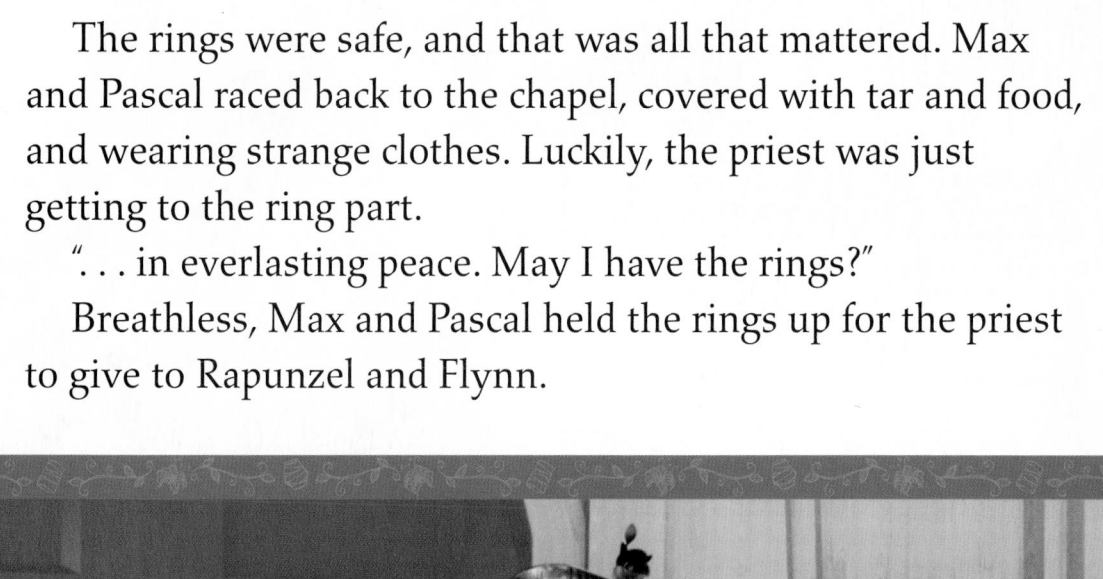

In the air, Pascal spotted a dove with the ring and stuck out his tongue. He caught the ring!

Max and Pascal finally both had their rings, but they still had not finished crashing into things. They didn't land on a flower cart or in a carriage, though. They fell through the roof of the tar works. Now they were covered in muck!

The wine barrels cracked open, and a huge flood of wine gushed down the street. Max ran away and rescued Pascal, whose lantern had landed nearby. Everyone else ran, too.

Max and Pascal came to a dead-end, but Max grabbed on to a line of flags from overhead and swung up and away from the flood.

Having been hit in the head so many times, Max felt dazed. His carriage banged into a wall at the edge of a large hill. Max went flying into the air again and landed on the street. A flower cart broke his fall.

Up above, one of the doves twirled Pascal's lantern around and around. The chameleon got dizzy and let go of the ring.

It pinged from one place to another until it landed on a hook holding a bunch of hanging barrels. They crashed down onto a mountain of wine barrels that had been stacked for the celebration.

As soon as the sky filled with doves, another group of royal workers looked up. "There's the doves. Release the lanterns!" The doves were their signal to start the next phase of the celebration.

Meanwhile, Pascal's lantern had gotten caught in the net, and he was able to climb on it and get his ring. But his lantern was floating, and by then, he was too high up to jump to the ground.

The crash sounded like a gong. Royal dove-keepers
heard it. They hadn't been expecting their cue so soon,
but they went to their stations at once. "That's the signal,
release the doves!"

Max was able to get a hold of his ring. Along the streets, merchants selling royal wedding souvenirs were lined up. They held out pans with a picture of Rapunzel and Flynn. "Frying pans! Commemorative frying pans here!"

The royal carriage was rolling so quickly that, because Max's head was sticking out, it banged into one pan after the next. And with a loud crash, he hit the frying-pan-warehouse sign.

The ring Pascal was chasing bounced down a sidewalk and into a paper lantern a little girl was holding. Shocked, she let it go.

It began to float toward a net that royal helpers were holding. The net covered a bunch of floating lanterns that were to be released as soon as Rapunzel and Flynn were married.

Max landed in the royal wedding carriage, which
was waiting to take Rapunzel and Flynn away. With all
the commotion, the ring had started rolling again. Max
chased after it in the carriage!

In the church, the priest continued the ceremony: ". . . held in reverence, dignity, honor, respect." Just as he said that, Max flew by the church window.

Luckily, everyone inside was paying attention to the ceremony so no one noticed.

Meanwhile, Max was chasing after the other ring, which was bouncing along the street. He ran so fast that he ran into the hair-and-makeup carts and ended up wearing a pink dress, a hat, and makeup. At last, the ring rolled to a stop under a cart.

Max almost had it! But just then, the ice sculpture landed on the other end of a cart. Max was catapulted into the air.

It again went from table to table, finally landing on one. Pascal stuck out his tongue to get it—and it stuck to an ice sculpture on the table. As the shocked chameleon yanked his tongue back, the ring went flying.

In the confusion, one of the servers bumped into the table and knocked the ice sculpture into the air.

The rings rolled onto a patio and over a wall down to the courtyard far below. Max and Pascal knew they had no choice. They jumped over the wall after the rings.

In the courtyard, hundreds of cooks and servers were putting the finishing touches on the food for the wedding banquet.

The rings went two ways, so Max and Pascal split up. One ring bounced from table to table, landing in a bowl of tomato soup. Pascal dove in after it and got it. But when he popped out of the bowl, he nearly gave a server a heart attack. *"Ahh!"*

He dropped the ring and away it bounced.

Only Max and Pascal had seen the rings fly away.

The priest continued the ceremony. "And the mutual respect which they bring to their life together."

Max and Pascal looked between the happy couple and the church door as the priest spoke. "The union of two people . . ."

Then they raced after the rings.

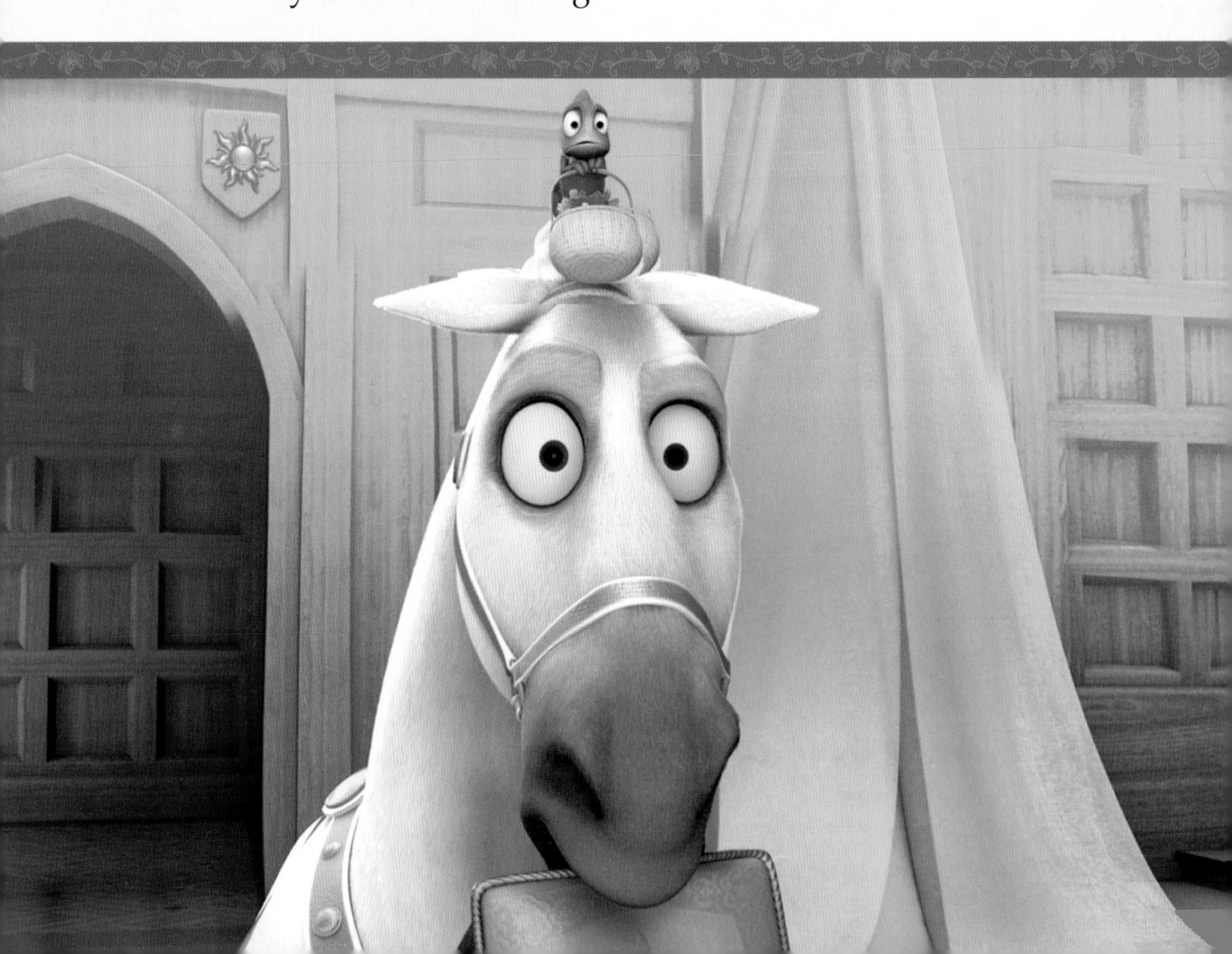

Max imagined the priest asking for them later in the ceremony. "May I have the rings?" Rapunzel and Flynn would be shocked. The whole castle would erupt in a panic. "The kingdom is lost!"

And the queen would be beside herself. First, she'd cry out: "Those were my grandmother's wedding rings!" And then, who knows? The wedding might have to be called off.

The flower tickled Max. He tried to ignore it, but he just couldn't.

A sneeze was coming! He did his best to stop it, but it was no use. "Ah-choo!"

As Max sneezed, the royal wedding rings sailed across the room and out the door!

The royal chapel looked beautiful. Every inch was filled with flowers. Rapunzel's parents, the king and queen, wanted everything to be perfect for their precious daughter's wedding.

When at last Rapunzel reached the altar, the ceremony began. "Dearly beloved, we are gathered here today to celebrate the joining . . ."

Pascal the chameleon and Maximus the royal guard horse stood at attention by their sides. As ring bearers, they shared a most important job. They smiled as they watched their friends beginning a new chapter in their lives. And then, all of a sudden, a flower drifted down . . . and landed on Max's nose.

Rapunzel was by far the loveliest bride the priest had ever seen. "Wow!"

She looked so beautiful that Flynn's heart skipped a beat. He was dazzled. "Wow!"

The day began when Flynn saw Rapunzel walk down the aisle. The whole church turned to admire the princess in her beautiful white dress and long, long veil.

"Everything was perfect—just like I always dreamed it would be!"

Flynn did have one complaint later, though—his portrait in the royal tapestry. "They *still* can't get my nose right."

Rapunzel reminded him of the wedding. "It was a magical day. And everything went just as we planned."

But Flynn knew that wasn't quite right. "Well, almost . . ."

It was the biggest celebration in the history of the
kingdom. Rapunzel always remembered it as a magical day.

Rapunzel was a long-lost princess who had recently returned to her kingdom. And in discovering who she was, she'd met and fallen in love with a former thief named Flynn Rider. After many adventures, Rapunzel and Flynn's wedding day arrived.

Read-Along
STORYBOOK AND CD

This is the story of Rapunzel and Flynn's royal
wedding. You can read along with me in your
book. You'll know it's time to turn the page
when you hear this sound. . . .

Let's begin now.

Printed in the United States of America
First Bindup Edition, June 2017
1 3 5 7 9 10 8 6 4 2

Library of Congress Control Number: 2016938190
FAC-008598-17111
ISBN 978-1-4847-8780-9

For more Disney Press fun, visit www.disneybooks.com

DISNEY PRESS

Los Angeles • New York

SUSTAINABLE FORESTRY INITIATIVE
Certified Chain of Custody
At Least 20% Certified Forest Content
www.sfiprogram.org
SFI-00993
Logo Applies to Text Stock Only